THE TOWN

and

THE COUNTRY

To Carol and Marianne

The version used in this book is based on the one found in *Select Fables of Esop and other Fabulists*, published by R. & J. Dodsley, Birmingham, England, 1764.

www.hmhbooks.com

Library of Congress Cataloging-in-Publication Control Number 75-141296

ISBN: 978-0-547-66854-3 paper over board

Manufactured in China
LEO   10 9 8 7 6 5 4 3 2 1

4500338899

THE TOWN MOUSE
AND
THE COUNTRY MOUSE

Paul Galdone

A FOLK TALE CLASSIC

Houghton Mifflin Harcourt

Boston   New York   2012

Once a contented country mouse
had the honor to receive a visit
from his old friend who lived at
His Majesty's Court.

The country mouse was extremely
glad to see his guest, and very
hospitably set before him the best
cheese and bacon, young wheat and corn
which his cottage afforded.

As for their beverage, it was
the purest water from the spring.

After supper, the two sat by the open hearth and chatted. "Really, my good friend," said the town mouse, "I am amazed that you can keep up your spirits in such a dismal place and with such rustic fare to eat.

"Truly you are wasting your time here.
Why, at court there is dancing and feasting and all kinds of merriment.
In short, there is never a humdrum moment.
But you must return with me tomorrow and see for yourself!"

The country mouse decided to sleep on it,
and told his guest he would give him his
answer next morning. Then they retired
in peace and quietness for a good night's rest.

The next morning when the guest
was ready to journey back to town,
he again urged his friend to accompany
him to His Majesty's Court. "Such
pomp and elegance and cuisine ought
not to be missed."

The country mouse finally consented
to go along, so the two friends set
out together.

It was late in the evening when they arrived at His Majesty's Court. And there, in the great dining hall, they found the remains of a sumptuous dinner.

There were creams and jellies
and sweetmeats, all of the
most delicate kind.
The cheese was the finest Parmesan
and they wetted their whiskers
with exquisite champagne.

But before they had half finished
their delightful repast,

they were greatly alarmed
by the barking and scratching of a dog.

Then the meowing of a cat
almost frightened them to death.

And then a whole army of servants
burst into the room
and cleared everything away in an instant.

The town mouse was by this time safe in
his hole—which, by the way, he had not
been thoughtful enough to show his
friend;
while the poor country mouse
could find no better shelter than that
afforded by the round leg of a sofa.
There he waited in fear and trembling
till quietness was again restored.

"Ah! my dear friend," said the country mouse
as soon as he had recovered enough to
have the courage to speak. "If your fine
living is interrupted constantly
with fears and dangers, let me return
to my plain food and my peaceful cottage.

"For what good is elegance without ease,
or plenty with an aching heart?"

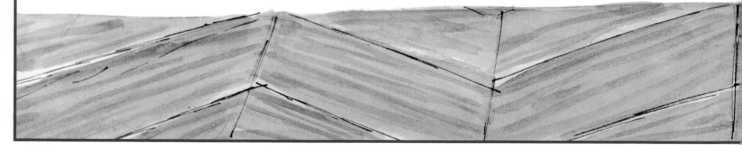

The town mouse asked his friend
to stay and spend the night.
But the country mouse said, "No, no.
I have seen enough of court life;
I shall be off as fast as I can."

And he ran out into the night . . .

. . . and did not stop until he reached
the peace and quiet of his cottage.